SPECIAL OFFERS FOR
LITTLE MISS READERS

In every Mr Men and Little Miss book you will find a special token.
Collect only six tokens and we will send you a super poster of your choice
featuring all your favourite Mr Men or Little Miss friends.

And for the first 4,000 readers we hear from, we will send you a
Mr Men activity pad* and a bookmark* as well – absolutely free!

Return this page with six tokens from Mr Men and/or Little Miss books to:
Marketing Department, World International Publishing, Egmont House,
PO Box 111, 61 Great Ducie Street, Manchester M60 3BL.

Your name:_____

Address:_____

_____

_____ Postcode: _____

Signature of parent or guardian: _____

I enclose **six** tokens – please send me a Mr Men poster ☐

I enclose **six** tokens – please send me a Little Miss poster ☐

We may occasionally wish to advise you of other children's books that
we publish. If you would rather we didn't, please tick this box ☐

*while stocks last   (Please note: this offer is limited to a maximum of two posters per household.)

Collect six of these tokens.
You will find one inside every
Mr Men and Little Miss book
which has this special offer.

1 TOKEN

Please remove this page carefully

MR MEN question time – can you help?

Thank you for purchasing this Mr Men or Little Miss pocket book. We would be most grateful if you would help us with the answers to a few questions.

Would you be interested in a presentation box to keep your Mr Men or Little Miss books in? **Yes** ☐ **No** ☐ (please tick)

Apart from Mr Men or Little Miss, who is your favourite children's character? _____

If you could write a Mr Men and a Little Miss book, what names would you give your characters? **Mr** _____

Little Miss _____

If applicable, where did you buy this book from? Please give the stockist's name and address.

Name: _____

Address: _____

_____

_____

THANK YOU FOR YOUR HELP

little Miss Chatterbox

by Roger Hargreaves

WORLD INTERNATIONAL
MANCHESTER

Little Miss Chatterbox talked more than a lot.

She talked all the time.

Day in and day out, week after week, month after month, year in and year out!

She never stopped!

She didn't know it, but she even talked in her sleep!

She had a brother.

I bet you can guess what his name was!

Can't you?

That's right!

Mr Chatterbox!

She looks a bit like him, don't you think?

You should have heard them when they got together!

You couldn't get a word in edgeways.

Or sideways.

Or anyways!

Have you ever heard about somebody being able to talk the hind leg off a donkey?

Well, Mr Chatterbox could talk both hind legs off a donkey.

And his sister could talk the hind leg off an elephant!

Now, this story is about the time little Miss Chatterbox decided to get herself a job.

Which she did.

In a bank.

In Happyland.

At ten o'clock one Monday morning Mr Happy strolled into the HappyToLendYou Bank in the middle of Happytown.

He took out his cheque book, wrote a cheque, and went to the counter.

Behind the counter, on her first morning at work, stood little Miss Chatterbox.

She smiled at Mr Happy.

Mr Happy smiled back.

"Good morning," he said, cheerfully.

"Well," said little Miss Chatterbox, taking a deep breath ...

"For the time of year it is a good morning but not as good as the morning we had yesterday and I dare say tomorrow morning will be an even better morning but it's quite a good morning for a Monday morning and ..."

And she went on and on and on until it was time for the bank to shut.

Mr Happy was still standing there, with his mouth open in amazement.

He'd been there for hours!

"And now," continued little Miss Chatterbox, "it's time for the bank to shut and time for me to go home so goodbye and nice talking to you and..."

And she went home, leaving poor Mr Happy without any money.

The following morning she was fired!

She got herself another job.

In a restaurant.

The Eatalot!

It was Tuesday morning, and at midday Mr Greedy walked into the restaurant and sat himself down at his usual corner table.

He always ate there on Tuesdays because that was the day they served extra large portions.

The waitress came up to take his order.

"What's the soup of the day?" Mr Greedy asked the waitress.

"Well," said little Miss Chatterbox, for she was the waitress. "The soup of the day is tomato but we also have other soups on the menu such as oxtail and vegetable and chicken and chicken noodle but we have lots of other things to start with such as..."

And she went on and on and on.

Until midnight!

Mr Greedy was still sitting there, listening, in amazement.

He'd been there for twelve hours!

Listening!

"And now," continued little Miss Chatterbox, "it's time for the Eatalot Restaurant to shut and for me to go home so goodbye and nice talking to you and..."

And she went home, leaving poor Mr Greedy feeling rather empty.

The next morning she was fired!

The same thing happened all week long.

On Thursday morning she was fired from her job as an assistant in a hat shop.

Miss Splendid went into the shop to buy herself a new hat, but she couldn't!

"Oh Madam I've just the hat for you and I know you're going to love it because it's pink and pink is your colour and it..."

It was all talk, and no hat!

On Friday morning she was fired from her job as a secretary to Mr Uppity.

Mr Uppity, incidentally, was the richest man in the world!

I just thought you'd like to know.

But poor Mr Uppity didn't make any money the day that little Miss Chatterbox was working for him.

Oh no!

"Oh Mr Uppity I've never worked in an office before and isn't it exciting and would you like a cup of coffee and are you as rich as everybody says you are and it..."

It was all talk and no work!

But, this story has a happy ending because at the very end of that week little Miss Chatterbox managed to find herself a job that suited her down to the ground.

And up to the sky!

That Saturday evening Mr Chatterbox was at home in Chatterbox Cottage.

Which was where he lived.

Mr Chatterbox was cross because his watch had stopped and he had arranged to meet little Miss Sunshine at seven o'clock and he had no idea what the time was.

So, he decided to telephone the Speaking Clock to find out what time it was.

He dialled the number.

"...at the third stroke it will be six twenty five and fifteen seconds!"

Little Miss Chatterbox took a deep breath.

PIP PIP PIP

"At the third stroke it will be six twenty five and twenty seconds!"

PIP PIP PIP

"That's funny," thought Mr Chatterbox to himself. "That sounds just like my sister!"